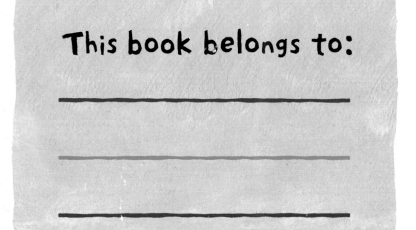

This book belongs to:

_____

_____

_____

First published 2003 by Walker Books Ltd
87 Vauxhall Walk, London SE11 5HJ

2 4 6 8 10 9 7 5 3 1

© 2003 Lucy Cousins
Illustrated in the style of Lucy Cousins by King Rollo Films Ltd

Lucy Cousins font © 2003 Lucy Cousins

"Maisy" audio visual series produced by King Rollo Films Ltd
for Universal Pictures International Visual Programming

Maisy™. Maisy is a registered trademark of Walker Books Ltd, London

Printed in China

British Library Cataloguing in Publication Data:
a catalogue record for this book is
available from the British Library

ISBN 0-7445-5767-4

www.walkerbooks.co.uk

Maisy's
Christmas Eve

Lucy Cousins

WALKER BOOKS
AND SUBSIDIARIES
LONDON • BOSTON • SYDNEY

Snow fell on
Christmas Eve.

Snow fell on
Maisy's house.

Snow fell on
Charley's
house.

Snow fell on
Cyril's house.

Snow fell on Tallulah's house.

Snow fell on Eddie!

He was on his way to see Maisy.

Everyone was invited to Maisy's house for Christmas.

Flip-flap!

Cyril went on snowshoes and got there slowly.

Swoosh! Swoosh!

Charley and Tallulah
went by sledge
and got there
quickly.

Plod-plop!
Eddie walked ...
and got stuck in
the snow!

At Maisy's house the snow fell thick and fast.
And it was ... COLD!
The friends hurried in to keep warm by the fireside.

Everyone got ready
for Christmas.

But where was Eddie?

They made mince pies, wrapped
presents and put
up paper chains.

But where was Eddie?

All together they decorated the Christmas tree.

But where was Eddie?

They all
went out
to look
for him.

They found a shed covered in snow.

But poor Eddie was stuck in the snow!

One, two, three... PULL!
One, two, three... PUSH!

Oh dear, Eddie was still stuck!

Then Maisy had an idea.
She fetched the tractor.

One, two, three ...

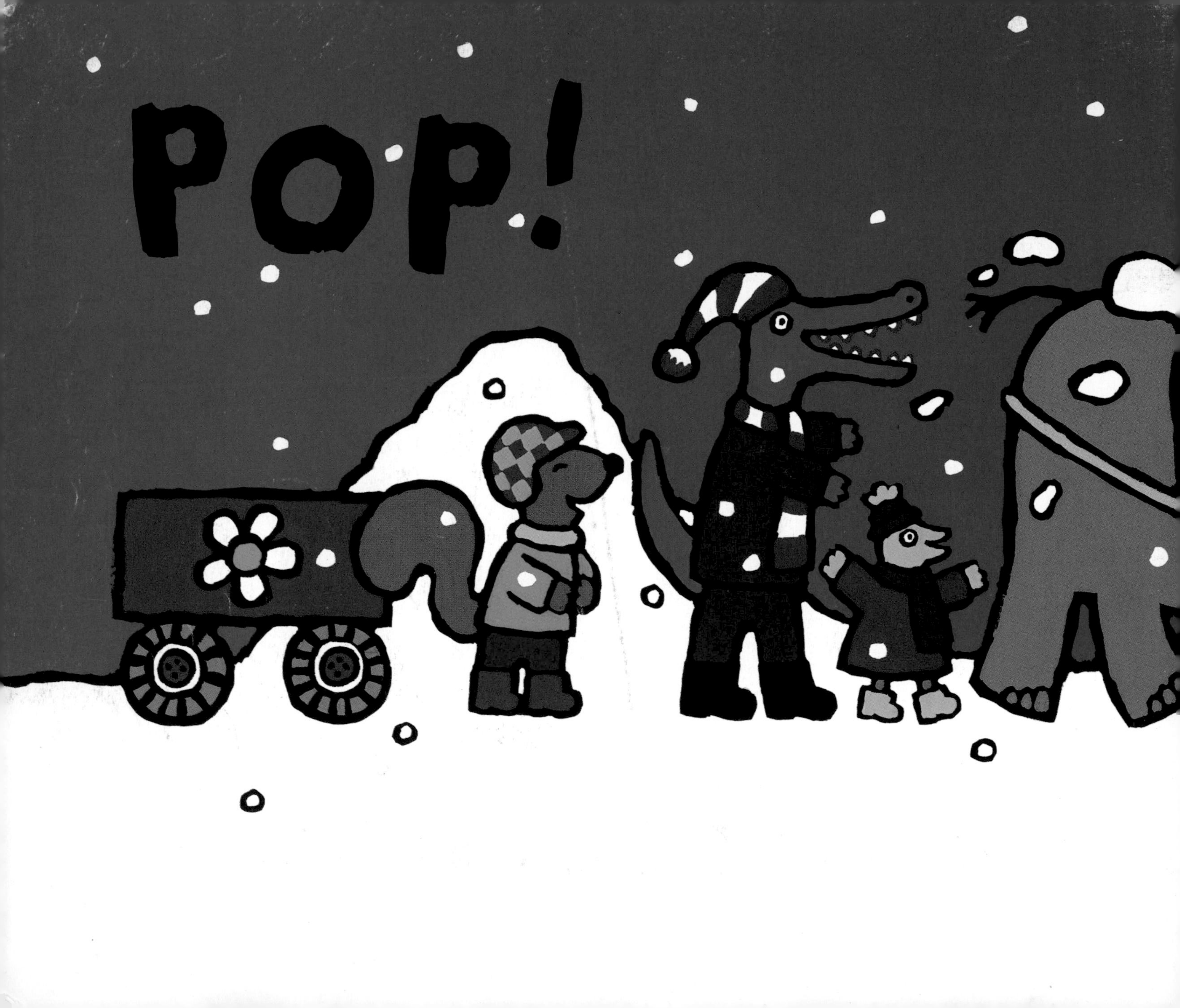
POP!

At last, Eddie was free.

That evening, everyone gathered around the tree to celebrate. Then the five friends sang Christmas carols together...

And Eddie sang
the loudest of all!